THE PRODUCERS

# Jack Felson's

# THE PRODUCERS

Two Colors

Published in 2011 by Two Colors Ventures, Ltd., London, United Kingdom

ISBN: 978-0-9565580-1-5

Printed and bound in the United States of America

## Introduction

This very short text was inspired to me by my own experience as a producer and investor hunter for my scripts, first in France, then in America and Canada, then back in France, then in UK – before I finally decided to self-publish and self-produce my works. It's rather difficult to rate it: the structure of this book makes it look like a novel, the abundance of dialogs and the total lack of psychology is screenplay-like, and the unity of place respects the first rule of stage plays. I first wrote it as a screenplay before a film producer told me that nobody would buy a ticket just to see two people talking in an office – and he was damn right. So I turned the script into this thing, without changing or adding anything, or almost. So please don't expect an action and romance-packed fiction story from this very special piece of storytelling, don't expect a remake of Mel Brooks' classic comedy either, this is only a little but accurate overview of the situation of cinema and film production today – nothing more.

*Jack Felson.*

A man is seated behind his desk, watching a movie on a laptop, with headphones on, while reading a film script. His first name's Alain. He's not making a sound.

Soon a door opens and another man appears. His name's Tony. Carrying a McDonald's package. Without saying hello, he walks to the other desk inside the room. He gets behind the desk and has a seat.

Still without saying anything, he opens the package and lays its content on the table. A salad, a Big Mac, a cheeseburger, a hamburger, a big Coca-Cola, a caramel sundae, etc. Then, he has a quick glance to the other man and, still without saying anything, he starts eating.

Alain is now watching the other guy, since he walked in. After a while he stops the film on the laptop, takes his head-phones off and puts the script on his table.

"Hey man, don't pay attention to me, please," Tony says.

"Are you?" Alain replies.

"Am I what?"

"Paying attention to me."

"To you? What d'you mean by that?"

"Don't you see? You get in here without knocking, without even saying hello or something, you go have a seat behind my partner's desk like it was your desk, and you start eating that smelly stuff from some fast-food, when it's not the right time."

"So? That's what I usually do."

"D'you all work like that in your country? Going out and coming in during work time, to get a coffee or hamburger at the closest McDonald's or something?"

"Yeah, exactly," Tony says, shrugging.

"Well, when I see that all the crises come from over there, I'm not surprised."

"Look, what's your problem? You're talking to me like to somebody you just met. We aren't strangers to each other."

"It's still the first time you show up in here."

"I'm just trying to do what I'm supposed to do. Making myself at home. What's with that?"

"You're not at home, and this is not your office. So please, show some decency."

"All right, all right. Where's your partner anyway?"

"He's in Belgium."

"What is he doing?"

"He's on a film project," Alain says. "Just like us."

"Right," Tony says, chuckling.

He keeps eating his 'lunch', slowly. Alain just keeps reading the script, but he doesn't put his headphones back on. Tony notices.

"What were you watching?" he asks.

Alain looks up.

"Sorry?"

"The laptop. What were you watching on your laptop?"

"A French film. You don't know."

"How d'you know about that?"

"I just know."

"Is it a DVD?"

"Yes."

"Can I see the cover?"

"Sure." Alain picks up the DVD cover, then: "Wipe your hands first."

"Just toss it."

"Wipe your hands."

"Shit," Tony says in a sigh. He starts looking for some towel around him, from the McDonald's bag. Nothing. "That bitch waitress didn't give me a towel."

"You mean you didn't take any."

"In my country the waiters give you a pile of towels along with your meal."

"Here in France they don't. You have to take the towels from the lobby."

"Stupid."

"So what do we do? I don't want you to spoil my DVD cover."

Tony looks at him for a short moment, saying nothing. Then: "Who are the actors?"

"Patrick Dewaere, Miou-Miou, Gerard Depardieu," Alain replies.

Tony shrugs again: "Never heard." He starts eating again, as Alain laughs up his sleeve. "What's so funny?" Tony asks, his mouth full.

"Nothing," Alain replies, still laughing.

Tony empties his mouth. "You think I'm an asshole because I don't know much about French stuff?"

"Believe me I don't. Anyway these days, most French films are stupid. You don't miss anything."

"Nice," Tony says, smirking. "So the movie you were watching is stupid as well?"

"Not that one. It's a movie from another time."

"I see. Are you hungry?"

"Yes. But I'll have lunch past noon."

"Look, forget about the time, okay? If you're hungry, don't bother yourself, just eat something."

"What d'you have?"

"I can give you my hamburger, if you like."

"All right."

Tony picks up the hamburger and

tosses it to him. Alain catches it and takes a couple of mouthfuls.

"What about the movie of yours?" Tony asked. "Don't you wanna watch it any more? You need me out?"

"I can watch it any other time," Alain replied, his mouth full.

"What is it about?"

"Two hoodlums and a chick," Alain answers after emptying his mouth, "riding away, talking about nothing but pussy and ass."

"That's a stupid logline."

"The movie is good anyway. You make the same kind of film today and it will be stupid."

"I don't agree. It depends who's invol-ved. I mean the crew and cast."

"It will be shit anyway."

"How can you be so sure?"

"I don't need to be sure. I just know."

"I think you're too nostalgic."

"Yes. I am, probably. I also believe there's too much money on the table these days. So we care about the quantity before the quality."

"Same thing."

"We think more about making big money than making good movies."

"You mean you think that way here as well?"

"Oh, yes."

"Look, I admit I don't know much about French cinema, but I think you're pushing here."

"Hey look, you guys from Hollywood don't have all the money in the world. We have some too."

"I didn't mean you French guys were all broke. Still…"

"Did you check the budget on this thing?" Alain asks, interrupting.

"This is an American project."

"French-American," Alain corrects. "With a French writer."

"So? Most of the money invested comes from the States. You can't deny that."

"This doesn't make it fully American."

"Okay," Tony says. "French and American."

"Remember, we're both working on this thing."

"I didn't forget."

"And there is a French investor involved."

"I won't forget that."

"Did you read that script?" Alain asks.

"Did you?" Tony retorts.

"Not yet."

"What?"

"I mean I haven't finished yet."

"What are you waiting for?"

"I didn't like what I've read so far."

"You like better scripts that have already been shot, right?"

"Did you read it?"

"Of course I did."

"And what do you think?"

"It's a piece of romantic shit."

This makes Alain guffaw. "So we understand each other," he says.

"What are we doing here, then?"

"There's much money on the table."

Tony says nothing right away. He's about to light a cigarette.

"You don't mean to smoke too, do you?" Alain reacts.

"Is it a problem?" Tony asks, as he lights the cigarette.

"It is for me."

"Sorry."

"You can use that ashtray."

The ashtray is on his table, he pushes it to him. Tony stands up, walks to Alain's table and extincts the cigarette.

Then he sees the DVD cover.

"*Les Valseuses*. What does that mean in English?" Tony asks.

" 'Balls', I guess," Alain replied. "Or 'nuts'. Something like that."

"Really?" Tony looks amazed, he shows wide opened eyes and mouth. Then he starts to laugh out. "Not bad. Not bad at all," he says as he walks back to his desk, still laughing.

He has his seat.

"You should be ashamed to give such titles to your films."

"This title doesn't sound crude in French," Alain says. "What do you care anyway?"

"We'd never do that in Hollywood."

"Sure you wouldn't. You guys are so prude. But I'm telling you again, that film is from another time, when things were more free. It wouldn't happen now."

"I see."

"I mean I believe it wouldn't happen now."

"You're not sure?"

"I'm no psychic."

"Of course not."

"And think about this too," Alain adds, "there's not as much censorship here as there is in your country."

"What d'you mean by that?"

"Well, for instance, the crude language is tolerated on TV. It's not automatically erased."

"Thanks."

"No offence. I've been in the States, I know what your TV looks like."

"Despite of that I guess your TV programs suck as well."

"That's right," Alain says, smiling. "But it's still more open. More real TV shit, for instance."

"What's the use, if the result is still shitty?"

"Good point. Guess what?"

"What?"

"Here most feature films are financed by TV channels."

"No shit?"

"No shit. They are in United Kingdom and most European countries as well. The French investor I mentioned works for one of those channels. As a matter of fact the channel itself is involved in this."

"That's right," Tony approves. "Er… 'TF1', right?"

"Right."

"Do you know the investor?"

"I've never met him."

"So how did you end up on this?"

"Simple. The writer submitted the script to me in the first place."

"Was it in French language?"

"Yes."

"What happened then?"

"Some months later he called me to

get some news. I admit I had totally forgotten about his work. I hadn't even had an eye on it. I had nothing to say to him so I suppose he submitted the script to a producer in America."

"That was me," Tony says.

"I don't think so."

"Just kidding. Actually he submitted his script to an agent in California. Who managed to sell it to a producer."

"Then you got involved," Alain concludes.

"The guy owed me a favour."

"He loved the story, tell me if I'm wrong."

"He did, but he didn't have the funding contacts. I knew somebody who could do something about it. Then we remembered the writer was French and this brought us to him, who told us about you."

"That's right."

"Nice guy. He didn't have to do that."

"Yeah."

"Can you explain me why French writers have more chances to succeed with producers in America than with those from their own country?"

"Don't ask me that."

"Why not? I'd like to know. I'm curious."

"Forget it. Anyway that's totally untrue."

"Yeah, I suppose that most French writers can't write in English."

"Right."

"That doesn't mean anything. Some of them still can. Have you ever talked to the writer?"

"No."

"You mean you've never talked with him? Even for a short interview?"

"In France we don't talk to writers. We never do."

Tony almost stands up from this. "You're crazy!" he said. "Why not?"

"We just don't," Alain just answers, shrugging.

"Well, that's stupid," Tony says, not believing his ears. "Now I kind of understand why your films are no much good." Alain doesn't say anything back right away. "In Hollywood the writer is considered the first step of filmmaking," Tony continued, "that's logical, he's the writer. He brings the material that will be used all along the process."

"Did you talk with him?" Alain asks.

"Of course I did. And not only me. Guess what? We even paid for his trip to us."

"Cool."

"What's your way with writers?" Tony questions. "What happens before a project is accepted?"

"Well, we do things rather like book publishers, you know. The writers mail their works to us, we review 'em, then we send a letter to the writer with a yes or a no."

"Wow. Great method," Tony says, grinning. "Did you send a letter to our guy?"

"I guess not."

"You need to wake up, fellows. You're not book publishers, but film producers."

"Same thing to me."

"You don't bring funding to the projects. Book publishers do that."

"They use all the same financing sources as we do," Alain retorts.

"Okay, let's make some thinking. Suppose you say yes to a project. You call or mail the writer to tell him, he's happy, etc. Then you start to look for the funding but after some long time you haven't found any source. How do you manage with the writer? What do you tell him?"

"Usually a producer here in France has his own funding sources. Just like you guys."

"You mean TV channels?"

"Not only that."

"Okay, but suppose the source, whatever it is, doesn't like the project and says no?"

"Then we try another one. Just like you guys. Same principle."

"And do you let the writer know?"

"Of course."

"In your opinion why do more and more of your writers and filmmakers come to us?"

"Maybe because you have more money."

"Maybe because we let them talk to us and be really part of the creative process. We do that right away, with no delay. The way you do things is a waste of time, in my opinion. Especially for the writer."

"Thank you very much," Alain says, "but we have made plenty of movies without your so valuable opinion and advice."

"Maybe, but the fact is you treat scripts like you wrote them yourselves. Because you don't talk to writers, you don't even wanna see them, I guess. In America things go totally different."

"Tell me more."

"Well, when a writer calls us we don't tell him to put his script in the mail and to wait for a reply that may never come. No. We let him come to us and we let him talk about his project."

"But you still have to read the script afterwards, right?"

"Sure. That's what scripts are written for. So we read them. But at least we already have a good idea about it. Because the writer gave it to us. This gives us a good and faster approach."

"Well, that's good for you. But this doesn't keep Hollywood writers from striking, right?"

"They do that for money and salary issues," Tony explains. "No connection."

"Why don't French writers strike, in your opinion?"

"Maybe because the union of writers here in France has no real power. Or because there isn't any. I don't know. You tell me."

"You're right, there isn't any."

"Wow. I suppose all the screenwriters here need to be directors too, right? Or else they'll never be successful."

"Just like in America."

"Wrong," Tony says back, opening round eyes. "Most of Hollywood directors haven't ever written a single script in their careers. Look at the Scott brothers.

Or Clint Eastwood. Or Ron Howard. Or David Fincher. Or Michael Bay. Guys like Hitchcock or John Ford have never written a damn thing in their lives. And most of screenwriters are screenwriters and nothing else. Especially when they work for TV. They don't need to direct to succeed and make a living. The thing is, the screenwriting job is recognized as a real profession in America."

"When it's not in France?"

"You tell me."

"You sound to know a lot about this matter."

"I'm a film producer, I make a living with the works from film writers. So yes, I'm supposed to know some about it. More or less. So you told me you haven't read the script completely. Among all the scripts you've received since you started your company, how many of them have you read completely?"

"It's not your business," Alain replies sharply.

"Okay. What's the use of telling writers to send you their scripts, if you let them pile up on your desk and in your closets without reading them?"

"Don't be silly. We do read the scripts we get in our mail."

"But you still didn't start to read this one before it reached a buyer in America. And you don't talk to writers. Not until they get some recognition I guess. So they need to turn into directors so they can be noticed, right? My conclusion, they don't need to submit their works to you guys."

"I don't know what you're talking about."

"Sure you do. All they have to do is produce and finance their first short films as directors themselves. Right? Then they show their movies in any ways available."

"Okay, okay. If you like."

"No. That's the point. You're not really interested in the scripts you get in the mail. You care more about the films you can see during festivals or whatever. Then you get interested in some film and you get in touch with the guy who did it. Am I wrong?"

"I think you're turning wild here. You're talking about me the same way you're talking about yourself."

"Why ain't you honest with all the writers who trust you? Why don't you tell them you don't really care about whatever they can write, as long as it's not on film?"

"Look, we do care of any material we can find, okay?" Alain says, a bit exasperated. "But like everybody else, a filmed material is more attractive. It is to you as it is to me."

"I've never said the contrary."

"This reminds me about a line in *Diary of the Dead* – did you see this movie?"

"George Romero," Tony nods, "yes."

"The line says: 'As long as it's not on film it doesn't exist.' That's perfectly true."

"Okay. This confirms what I said. Scripts don't exist to you as long as they're not filmed. The fact is you don't do much for them to end up on film."

"You can't say that," Alain says, shaking his head. "You don't know nothing about it."

"It's still up to the writer more than it is to you."

"Of course. It's his project."

"So he doesn't really need you."

"Of course he does! I'm here to produce his project. To make it possible and done, to find the money for that."

"Give me the right to doubt it."

"Sure you can. You're so different."

"Our writer still had to come to us to find a producing crew."

"So what? Can one single case give you the right to say that we don't do our job correctly? And that all French writers should try their lucks elsewhere?"

"If all the French writers could write in English they'd all work in Hollywood right now."

"Soon you'll tell me that the screen-writers in America are all successful and part of the system."

"You believe that leaving the writer on his own is a solution?"

"Of course not."

"So we're not that different. We think the same way…"

"…but we don't do things that same way."

"That's right."

"The result is the same: we both make films."

"Of course. But it takes more time for you to do it. As it takes much more time to your creators to be part of your system, than it does to ours."

"How can you be so sure about that?"

"It's easy to guess. The average age for a starting filmmaker in the States is 23. When Sam Raimi made *The Evil Dead,* he was only 18, you know. Can you give me an example of a French director who could start making feature movies that young?"

"I'll think it over."

"You won't find any. I can take the bet."

"Possibly."

"Tell me about the producing process here in France. Why are TV channels involved in film financing?"

"Look, I didn't create the system, all right? Why not, anyway? I don't see where the problem is."

"I'm intrigued. It doesn't make sense. Don't you use money from investors, or hedge funds, or… or banks?"

"We don't have the big studios you have, all right? Even if there's one on its way in the suburbs of Paris."

"Yeah? Who's behind it?"

"Luc Besson. D'you know him?"

"Who doesn't? I've seen some of the last films he did as a producer. Kind of inspired by some of our stuff, if not taken from them. So this guy's about to be the first French movie nabob, right?"

"The first French Hollywood-style movie nabob, yeah. He's also about to poison the French cinema with his storytelling and business vision imported straight from your big studios. Because of him the film budgets here will increase like crazy, as they do in Hollywood, and we'll have to put gloves on before opening a script."

"What are you so afraid of? There are studios like ours in Canada, you know, and in Rome, too. The Cinecitta, I guess. Also in India. Lars von Trier recently opened a big studio in Denmark, and there's a big movie studio about to open in Venezuela. Why not in Paris?"

"There's been a Eurodisneyland around Paris for a while, soon there's gonna be a 'Eurollywood'. Or 'Frenchywood'. And we'll all become fat stupid Americans for good."

"There's still much time before you get all the major studios we have. And you believe the money we put in our films comes from the studios?"

"Doesn't it?"

"Look, let me tell you this: the major Hollywood studios are nothing else than film production companies. They're big, I won't say they're not, but they're still film production companies. Just like any film production company here. And each one of these companies has its own investors."

"So you just go get the money from where you can find it. Just like we do. The difference is, we don't have investors being part of our companies. They're outside. That's what makes them not be called film studios."

"Why are your products called motion pictures when they're financed by television?" Tony asks.

"Because they are shot on film or digital stuff, and end up in theaters. What, you think the money from TV is different from the one not from TV?"

"Of course not. Your problem, when you let a TV channel finance your film project, in the end you let the channel get involved in the filmmaking process, and the result may look like a TV series episode more than a real film. Don't you think so?"

"I don't have an opinion on that."

"Don't you watch any of the films that were released here recently?"

"Of course I do."

"And don't you have anything to say about the directing, style and aesthetics?"

"I don't care about that. That's not my line."

"Not your line, huh?"

"Yeah, exactly."

"Then why do you find today's French movies so silly, if you don't care about the way they're done? Why do you show so much 'nostalgia' "?

"That's the point. I'd be more interested in the style of today's French films if it was more exciting."

"Yeah. I kind of see what you mean. Hey, do you remember what happened in 2004, during the Cannes Film Festival, when Michael Moore won the Palme d'Or for *Fahrenheit 9/11*"?

"What exactly happened?"

"Well, some people, I guess they were French, told the president of the jury that the movie was not fiction, so it was not what we call cinema, and it had no right to be awarded. Especially with the Palme d'Or."

"Yeah, I remember that."

"Problem is, the film was produced by a major studio."

"What are you talking about that for?"

"I'm just curious, that's all. Why do some French folks argue about a non-fiction film receiving the highest award at the biggest film festival in the world, when their own fiction films are produced by TV channels?"

"Look, there are jerks everywhere. And *Fahrenheit 9/11* wasn't even the first non-fiction film getting the Palme d'Or at Cannes."

"Exactly," Tony approves. "And that first one was a French movie."

"Don't you finish your lunch? It's gonna get cold."

"There's a micro-wave outside," Tony says, shrugging.

"It doesn't work."

Tony starts eating his Big Mac. "I had to mention this because the president of the jury was Tarantino," he says with his mouth full, "that made it ironic as hell." He empties his mouth. "Don't you finish the hamburger?"

"No." Alain throws it into a basket.

Tony keeps eating his Big Mac. He finishes it, then he has some Coca-Cola. "D'you want some?" he asks.

"No."

"Jesus, you're a maniac."

"I'm French. I care about what I eat."

"I can see you do."

"Less and less French people do, you know."

"What d'you mean?"

"Your fast-food system is spreading across France now. Up to the best classical restaurants."

"Really?"

"Really. Soon we'll all be as fat and badly fed as you are."

"Too bad. Okay let me say this: if you don't care about the way French films are done, then you're disappointed about something else in them."

"Yeah? What?"

"The way they've been written, what d'you think?"

"Possibly. But in general, I find French movies rather poor on a visual point of view. And yes, most of them are based on lousy scripts."

"I've read somewhere that there are no agents for screenwriters in France. Is that truc?"

"I have to admit it, yes."

"And don't you think *that*'s the problem?" Tony asks.

"What d'you mean?"

"You do know what I mean. And it also confirms what I've already said, that French writers need to turn into directors in order to give themselves the best chances to find their scripts on the screen. Only a small part of them manages to do it, and they're not necessarily the best writers."

"That's an interesting point."

"Since they can't find an agent to represent them, the screenwriters here don't have much choice, right?"

"I guess so."

"They need to be directors too, or to send out their works over the Atlantic. Don't you find this terrible?"

"You've already said that before, and I can't help it."

"Sure you can, you're a producer. Yes or no?"

"I'm not an agent."

Tony nods. "Yeah, there's no such thing here anyway."

"I can see you're really concerned about the situation here. Thank you."

"I just don't understand it."

"But you can't help it either. So forget about it, okay? I've been in the States before as I told you, and the situation there didn't look any better to me."

"The problem in Hollywood is the money. There's too much dough invested in film projects now. This makes the fields of possibilities narrower and narrower."

"That's correct," Alain approves.

"But at least the creators have the possibility to show their works to producers like us, with a pretty good chance to sell them. And they have the possibility to talk, too."

"For what result? If the work is an original story, it has more chances to be rejected."

"It still can be sold. I guess there is no producer in France able to buy a script, right? Especially if the writer shows up without an agent along."

"I believe our writer was very lucky to find buyers."

"In the States we buy scripts every day. I don't see where the miracle is."

"When I see how budgets are increasing and all the copies that are produced in Hollywood today, you know, sequels, remakes and whatsoever, how systematically they are being released, it's quite obvious to me that you guys don't really care any more about original things, even if you pretend to do so."

"We don't pretend to do anything. We care about all the projects, especially when they're fresh. But as the budgets always get higher and higher, we also need to care about 'bankability'. Same as you. Why shouldn't we?"

"So what else do you need before you accept a project?"

"What else? We don't need a lot. Only a story to be good."

"That one sucks to you."

"I'm not the one who bought it. The guy who did found it good. Everyone to his taste."

"Don't you need a story to have some commercial potential too?"

"Yeah, sure."

"I bet it's the very first thing you need to find in a story."

"You bet."

"What's if you find a story good but not commercially attractive?"

"We can hire some other writer to adjust it."

"A writer from the inside, I suppose?"

"You suppose correctly."

"I figured."

"What would you do?"

"We'd ask the original writer to adjust it himself."

"Really? I thought you didn't talk to writers."

"We may do that when the project is kind of accepted."

"Of course."

"No shit. What about this one? Has it been adjusted?"

"I guess not."

"Does it have some potential to you, as it is?"

"It's crap to me, but it's a romance story, and I guess because it's a romance, it has a good commercial potential. Look at *Love Story,* this movie is very bad, but it worked very well."

"I see. So you intend to do the same with this?"

"If you say so. Even if I've never thought about it this way."

"Really?" Alain says, unconvinced.

"You'll have to ask your question to the producer who bought this."

"Do you always get involved in projects you don't find interesting?"

"When there's much money on the table, I don't mind."

"I see."

"I'm just using your words," Tony specifies.

"I know."

"But I won't tell anything on this about filmmaking, if you wanna know."

"Sure you won't, it's not part of your job."

"Don't worry, most producers and executives do mind about filmmaking in Hollywood."

"I know, and they shouldn't."

"You can say that from where you are, but if you were over there, with your money invested in some big project, believe me you would mind."

"If I was some executive I'd invest my money in a project and director I fully trust. I wouldn't invest my money only for the pleasure to force my opinion and be a pain in the director's ass."

"This is very nice," Tony says ironically.

"It's not about being nice, but about being realistic. How's the use about being a film director in Hollywood if you can't put what you want in the frame?"

"The director doesn't bring the money."

"But it's still *his* project. I mean it's supposed to be his project, right? And only because he doesn't allow it to be started, and no matter how hard he fought to find a financing and producing crew, it's no longer his project, he doesn't even have the final cut."

"I don't see why you're complaining, you don't work in Hollywood."

"I'm not complaining," Alain corrects, "I'm just reacting the same way you did about screenwriters. And guess what, I've kind of thought about going to L.A. I guess every French artist and producer thinks about going somewhere else, especially in Hollywood, to make more money and be better off in the business."

"How d'you think about it now?"

"I don't know. I guess if I was in Hollywood I'd still let a director do whatever he wants, no matter how much money is invested on his project."

"Good for you."

"So you kind of agree with me, with the way I produce films?"

"Not really," Tony replies, shaking his head, "no. I think I told you how."

"You think it would be suicidal?"

"Especially if there's no famous actor involved. It would be like nailing your own coffin."

"I'm crazy but not that much. Of course I'd help the director to find names, it's part of the producer's job anyway."

"Look, in Hollywood, we have an approach of film that is commercial first."

"I know that. I see your blockbusters."

"It's all about making good profit, okay?"

"Yeah, but not only that. It's also about making good films, you know. *Cinema.*"

"Of course. Give me the perfect script, add to it a couple of famous actors and a director that can be trusted, and the movie will exist."

"Yeah, but the question is, how deep will you be involved in filmmaking, and will you let the director do whatever he wants without arguing all the time about this and that?" Alain says.

"About what, for instance?"

"You know what. Violence. Or bad language. Or morality. Or shooting delays. Stuff like that."

"Oh please, don't tell me that you French guys don't talk about those matters when you make a movie!"

"Now I can see you don't watch French stuff. You should attend some film shootings here, you could be surprised. In general the producers and funders are not on set."

"Really?"

"Exactly. The director is the boss, he does what he's supposed to do: direct. Without anybody behind to tell him how to do things and how he wants them done."

"That's cool."

"You also should watch French TV. You'd be surprised about the way things are showed, you know. No censorship, we use signs instead."

"Signs?" Tony asks, not understanding.

"Symbols. We put them on the screen. For kids."

"I see."

"When they see that symbol, they change the channel, or their parents do it for them, and that's it."

"Not bad. So you don't have to cut in the programs."

"We don't even have to change them."

"Hey, not so fast, we don't do that!" Tony protests.

"Of course you do! What about crude language, like the 'F' word? Don't tell me you don't do anything about it! You US TV guys never hesitate to re-edit others' films and change whatever you don't like in any program, especially when it's a film or a real TV show. I know about the way you treat Jerry Springer's guests. I also know about the way your TV keeps treating films like *Scarface* or *Reservoir Dogs,* or *Do the Right Thing.*"

"Wow. Now I understand why the tourists from the US find the French so unpleasant."

"Yeah, we do speak the way we want, with no restraint. And in the same time we're more liberal, you know, for instance we don't change film contents on TV only in order to make them lighter. There's a name for that, 'free expression'. You can't blame us for it, it's part of your Constitution I guess. And we still don't call you names, right?"

"I guess you don't."

"So that's the way we do things and it does work, you know. However crude and unpleasant they may be, kids and teenagers here in France are far less dangerous than they can be in the States. They don't have guns on them anyway. I suppose you know that. You won't get shot or assaulted on our streets."

"Haven't you been some tour guide before in your life or what?"

"No. I just saw *Bowling for Columbine.*"

"Very funny."

"And I've been in the States too."

"Let's get back to our movies, okay?"

"Sure. Just wanted to show you that here in France we don't need any official censorship and image control to try to make things better."

"I'll write it down somewhere."

"Don't forget to tell your friends too. I didn't forget what you said about this." Alain shows Tony the DVD cover. "It's the title of a very well-known film in France, but it didn't turn everybody hysterical you know, sex and cunt crazy."

Tony smiles. "I can see it didn't drive you mad," he says, "sure thing."

Alain puts the DVD down. "It didn't drive anybody nuts here in France, I'm telling you," he confirms. "You know what I think?" he adds. "I think you American people are scared to death."

"Are you thru? We still didn't get back to our movies."

"Okay, I quit. Did you see *The Player*?"

"*The Player*? No."

"Too bad. I guess it's the kind of film you Americans don't watch."

"Who is this from?"

"It's from Robert Altman, you know, one of those great US directors who never had the Oscar. And the main characters in this film are producers in Hollywood. The beginning shows some of them talking with screenwriters, in private, inside their office."

"Inside the studios?"

"Yes."

"Of course. That's the way things work over there."

"Later on another scene shows one of them giving the idea of taking the screen-writer away from the artistic process."

"Really? That's a bit exaggerated."

"Certainly not. This movie came from the inside."

"I'll have to see that one."

"The thing is, most producers reason like they are the screenwriters and the directors."

"Wrong, they reason like the business-men they are. And you know what, the fact is, most directors in Hollywood are also producers. You know, they are kinds of businessmen too. Look at Spielberg."

"They have to, to keep control on their work. Because they know that they won't have the final cut if they don't produce.

And because mainstream producers don't have any culture of cinema, they're just here for the money."

"Are you always that nice when it comes to Hollywood?"

"Again it's not about being nice but…"

"…but about being realistic," Tony finishes, "yes, I know."

"And because those nabobs have the money, they believe they know better than the screenwriter and director. But the question is: if they are so smart, why don't they take their places? Why don't they take the camera and direct their movies themselves?"

"Because they are nabobs, not film-makers, that's why."

"Yeah, so they just need to take film-making classes and that's it."

"Yeah, and why don't they do that?" Tony asks.

"Because they are too stupid or too lazy, that's why. And it's these dumb guys who control the real creators and make the decisions."

"Yeah, that's what they do, so they can't be filmmakers in the same time."

"Some of them do it anyway."

"You seem very well informed."

"No, it's all about being logical. And about control. So there must be producers over there, who turn into directors just for the purpose of controlling all the film-making process, for the film to fit their commercial vision."

"No. I'll tell you what they do. They look for directors whose works may fit their commercial vision and they hire them, put them under contract. Or they train them to do that. You see what I mean?"

"Kind of, yes."

"Look at, for instance, producer Jerry Bruckheimer and director Michael Bay, that's a good example. There are other duos like that, all across Hollywood. The nabob and the yes-man."

"Yes, I see. Are you happy with that?"

"I can't tell. I don't see Michael Bay's films."

"You don't want to, or you didn't have the chance?

"Both, I guess. Did you have the chance to see any of what he recently did as a producer?"

"Because he's a producer now?" Alain asks.

"Yes. When he doesn't direct pointless blockbusters under Bruckheimer's wing, he turns himself into a shark producer, making very standard remakes of American horror classics. Like *The Texas Chainsaw Massacre,* or *Amityville.* Or recently *A Nightmare on Elm Street.* Only remakes of famous scary films, it's safer I guess. He also produced a prequel to *Massacre!* He's become himself a factory for that kind of stuff. And he's found himself a bunch of yes-men for that. Especially a director from Europe. From Germany, to be more specific."

"I see. Would you like to be one nabob's puppy?"

"I'm not a filmmaker, I'm a producer."

"Suppose you were a director, would you like to be under the orders of some big shot producer?"

"I don't think so."

"You see."

"Now wait a minute. There's one thing you don't seem to understand. Every time we put money on a film we take a big risk."

"Thanks, I understand that, that's what I also do, as well as every producer in France and all over the rest of the world."

"Yeah, but it's more true in Hollywood than in any other place. It's like gambling, you know, playing roulette, and the amounts on stake are way bigger."

"Of course it's especially true in Hollywood. And you know why? Because now you no more hesitate to give a 40-million-dollar check to one actor, for him or her to only play in one movie. For me that's where you play roulette and put your heads on stake."

"Hey, you should say that to those who can afford to do that, all right?"

"Are you a Hollywood producer, yes or no?"

"I'm not a nabob," Tony says. "And I'm talking about all the producers, so don't count me in the nabob part. Please."

"You still work for a major studio," Alain insists.

"That doesn't mean I'd waste that much money on one head. We are not all the same, you know."

"Then explain me why the average budgets in Hollywood always get bigger and bigger?"

"Are you trying to make me responsible for this whole damned situation?"

"You're part of the system that created that situation."

"And I can't help it, and I'll tell you, we producers can't help it. That's just the way it is."

"Of course."

"That's right. You're talking about us as greedy businessmen, but what about the others' greed? Actors', for example."

"That's gonna be the actor's fault, now!"

"I didn't say that. But they have a great part of responsibility in the non-stop increase of budgets today. We can't control their financial desires."

Alain disagrees: "Of course you can," he says. "All you have to do is say 'no' and that's it. End of story."

"It's not that simple. We can say anything we want to screenwriters and directors and make them do whatever we want them to do. But we just can't do that with actors, you know, with the stars. They got us."

"Bullshit!"

"Hey, who are you to say no to me about that?" Tony says, kind of upset. "I think I have the best position to talk here."

"What about the 50-million-dollar check Johnny Depp recently got for *Pirates of the Caribbean 4*? Are you gonna tell me that he demanded that without negotiating? I don't think so. He was given that whole pile of money very graciously, from you guys."

"Maybe, but the fact is we can't control actors like we can control writers and filmmakers. We can tell writers and directors about how we want a script to be written and a film to be filmed, but we can't tell an actor about how he's suppo-sed to play. Especially when it's a movie star. That's the director's job."

"So?"

"So? Since we don't tell them how to do their job we don't have anything to tell them about their salaries either. They can tell us whatever they want about that."

"Oh come on! Don't tell me you'd be the movie stars' puppies?"

"I won't go that far."

"You're in charge, yes or no? I mean, the producers, the executives?"

"Yes, but when a film achieves great box-office success, it's mainly thanks to the star, of course he or she knows it, and that gives him or her much power, more than you can imagine. Look at Tom Cruise, you believe this guy has no power? And who d'you think makes the rules on a blockbuster's shooting set? It's not the director, it's not even the producer or the executive. It's the actor, I mean the star. He, or she, is the one who makes the rules and gives the orders."

"And he or she decides about his or her own paycheck too?"

"Of course we always negotiate, but just try to see me facing Stallone or Bruce Willis, or Tom Hanks, or Mel Gibson about that, who d'you think will win in the end?"

"If things really go that way on your films, then I pity you."

"We don't need that, but thanks anyway."

"And now, I can suppose that when you guys try to impose your commercial vision and rules on a filmmaker when he just wants to make cinema, you know, to do what he was trained for, you understand what he may feel about it."

"If you think I'll start having insomnia about that, you're greatly wrong."

"I know somebody who'd be very happy to hear that," Alain says.

"You mean the director?"

"Yeah, of course."

"Oh, are you gonna tell him? If you like I can call him right away."

"So you'll tell him."

"No, I'll bring him here so you tell him."

"No, you will. Your words, not mine. Face to face. It could be funny."

"Okay. Why not, after all?" Tony takes his cell phone. "What's his number?"

"It's on the script."

Tony finds the number and dials it. "Hello, Mr. Coons?" he finally says in the phone. "Yeah, it's Tony Meldon, the producer. I'm in Alain's office. He's here too. Could you come over, please? We'd both like to talk to you." A pause. "Yes, right away. All together. Is it possible?" A pause. "We'll tell you when you show up." A pause. "Okay, good. We'll be waiting." He cuts.

"Is he coming?" Alain asks.

"Yes."

"Did you really talk to him?"

"Sure, why?"

"I didn't hear anything coming from your phone."

"Of course, I didn't turn the loud speaker on."

"Still..."

"Okay, I pretended. You're happy?"

"That's why I thought."

"Let's come back to our beloved actors. Did you notice anything about the cast?"

"Sure. No stars."

"That's right. And that's cool. I mean, better."

"Why aren't there any stars involved?"

"We didn't need any. We spent months and months trying to get just one, in order to start it for good. We never could, so we just dropped. And we had to do that to realize that we really didn't need any."

"Yeah." Alain doesn't look convinced.

"I told you, the story has enough potential to be able to be shot without names. Celebrity is not a must on this. Let's take *Love Story* again, as an example. D'you think Ali McGraw was famous before that movie? No, she was almost a beginner. And before that film, Ryan O'Neal was working for television, on lousy series."

"So? That was 40 years ago. When movies cost shit to studios. Now they cost their asses."

"That's one of the two reasons I finally didn't try to get names involved. Waste of time and money. You know the other reason."

"D'you think we don't trust stories any more?"

"Don't you agree with that? You were talking about all the copies that are released in chains today, like from a factory. Remakes and stuff. Here we go. You're perfectly right. Anyway trying to get funding from classical investors is too complex and frustrating today."

"Everything depends on movie stars, right?"

"Almost everything," Tony approves. "Today, no matter how good, original and fresh a story can be, it's no more enough to get the project started. Far from it. And that's where things turn very difficult and exhausting for us producers. And that's one of the reasons some directors from the 60's and 70's believe that the real cinema is dead. The good old days are finished, they're behind us. I've already told you about the amazing power a movie star can have these days, that power is the very point here. As you probably know, most of the actors, especially when they are popular, and their agents expect a project to be already fully financed, with the paycheck ready to be cashed, no matter how good or bad the story is, they don't really care. And on the other hand, the investors expect the same project to be already fully casted, with at least one or two big movie stars involved, and you know how hard they are to get. If you consider that situation, you'll see that you can't do anything good and get anything much, especially if you don't have any personal money to invest or if you can't borrow any by yourself, you're going straight to the wall. It's very frustrating, and with the films getting always more expensive it's getting worse and worse."

"I see," Alain says. "One way or the other you're stuck."

"But the stars are not always necessary. You don't need them when you only 'remake' cinema classics, in order to turn them into regular blockbusters, or when you pick up materials for the young, like videogames or comic books, or novels like *Harry Potter* or *Narnia,* or *Twilight,* you see, any stuff that is already internationally popular, and put it on the screen. There, we don't use movie stars, 'cause we don't have to. The marketing point is the popular material. But that includes rights that are as hard to get for us, and almost impossible to get for indie producers."

"We don't see things that way here."

"I know, I guess movie stars here are not crazy, they don't want Fort Knox."

"The biggest movie star here makes $2 million a movie, maxi."

"In Hollywood, despite all the dough they can make, the actors still find ways to go on strike."

"That's not surprising," Alain says. "As you know the actors, especially in Hollywood, have the reputation of being the most pretentious people in the world."

"And I suppose you're smart enough to explain me why they're so pretentious?"

"Sure. By dint of seeing all those big movie projects that are built on their famous names, in the end they believe that the whole world turns around them."

"If you were offered the opportunity to blow up the whole city, you would take it right away, ain't I right?"

"Ain't I right?" Alain asks.

"You don't need to say such vexing things."

"But they're true, aren't they?"

"I have to admit it, yeah."

"You know what? What I just said is also valid here, in France. About French actors."

"Really?"

"Yes. The only difference, the actors have no real power."

"I believe you."

"You better believe me, because it's true. But think about it, if the French actors don't get any power, it's simply because they don't deal with production."

"Oh, you mean that…"

"In the United States, there are many actors who are also producers, who have their own production companies, right?"

"Yeah, plenty of them."

"Well, in France, you won't see such people."

"I see. Lazy bastards, right?"

"Not really. They just stay seated, waiting for scripts to fall down on their knees from the sky, instead of working themselves on new projects. But I kind of understand them, you know. It's because of the production system, it's too complex. There are too many institutions involved, too many intervening parties, the TV channels included. And none of these parties will get involved into a project as long as it doesn't have a financing proof from any party, whatever it is."

"A real jungle," Tony says.

"Yeah, like a never-ending circle. Anyway it's too heavy to handle. I suppose the actors know it, so they don't wanna deal with it. They do acting and that's it. Being an actor in France is cushy. Being a producer in France is like being in hell. Really."

"Nobody keeps you from looking for another job."

"No thanks. In France, the producers do all the hard and dirty work, yes. But that allows us to stay in charge and to pay the actors the way we want, without being answerable to them."

"I understand."

"Don't you think you guys are too obliging?"

"The nabobs are, yeah. They can't help it, me neither. What about producers here in France?" Tony asks. "Don't you think they're kind of becoming like us, in spite of all the hard work they have to do?"

"Oh, they're on their way to be as obliging as most of Hollywood producers may be. You can see that in some films, especially those that are produced by Luc Besson. Look at *The Transporter*. Did you see that one?"

"No."

"It's a series of French big films, written and produced by Besson, with a Hollywood action movie star on top. That's the kind of movie that could have been produced in Hollywood. When I saw the first installment I thought I was watching some Jackie Chan movie mixed with *The Fast and the Furious* and *Die Hard*. It's fast, filmed like some MTV music video, with some invulnerable guy who can escape from anything and face anybody with no problem, with many stunts and fight scenes, beautiful, powerful vehicles and a pretty lovable chick he keeps running after for her safety. No real story, no psychology at all. And we call that a form of expression. I don't. If Besson intends to keep producing such empty films through his coming studios, and I think he does, we'll have enough to be afraid of."

"All right, but do you think that all French producers will become like him?"

"When his studios are open, many of them will work for him. And he won't no more be the only one to produce fast popcorn movies like *The Transporter* or

*Ong-Bak,* or *Taken.* Everybody will get to it."

"Are you concerned about that?"

"I don't know if I have to be. We'll see. What about you?"

"What?"

"Are you concerned about Hollywood?" Alain asks.

"Hollywood will break down soon of course, everybody knows it, so I have no reason to be concerned about it. If the system doesn't break down all by itself, a big earthquake will do it for it. And when it happens, you'll be still standing, whatever Besson does. And you'll take over."

"D'you really mean that?"

"Yes. With the budgets always getting bigger, and the movie stars always racing for the biggest paycheck ever, we can't get away. Being a producer in Hollywood is always more difficult and frustrating because of all this waste."

"Nothing keeps you from looking for another job," Alain suggests.

"No, thank you."

They grin together.

"You certainly know they've started to downsize their staffs," Alain restarts.

"I do."

"So who knows? Maybe in some months from now you'll be on the streets, without even having to quit."

"Yeah, who knows," Tony says, chuckling.

"So about this thing, I suppose you don't think about it as a blockbuster?"

"I don't. Only as a romance, which can become a hit."

"Today the audience wants action first."

"Not the total audience. A good part of it wants to feel good first. Nothing better than a love story with a happy ending."

"Don't be too sure about that. If you

take *Titanic,* it's a love story that doesn't end happily."

"Yeah, that's the reason they added that final scene, you know, the Heaven of the Titanic or something like that, to give us the illusion of a happy ending, and it worked. Anyway *Titanic* is a good example of a big film that didn't base its success on the cast. The important point was the story. That historical background around the ship, and a love story that evolves well. DiCaprio became a superstar only after the highly successful release."

"Don't dream too much anyway. The budget on this isn't that high."

"$45 million, it's nothing to you?"

"It's nothing compared to $200 million. But I admit it, it's a lot compared to the budget on *Love Story.* That's not good."

"Wait and see," Tony proposes.

"And there's no legendary stuff around that romance here anyway."

"There's no such thing in *When Harry met Sally* and *Love Story,* either. Don't be too demanding."

"Okay."

"And we're not trying to do as well as *Titanic,* right? I'm not dreaming."

"That's the reason you won't bother the director on set."

Tony shows an odd smile. "All things considered, maybe I will. Maybe it will be worth it."

"I figured."

"Have you produced any romantic stuff before?" Tony asks.

"Yes, sure. With more or less luck."

"I suppose it's your first experience as a co-producer, on a project like this?"

"Yes."

"And you still didn't read the script completely? That's too bad."

Alain shrugs. "I guess so."

"What do you expect from this first Hollywood experience?"

"I don't know."

"You speak English very well. How long have you been speaking English fluently?"

"For a couple of years."

"And since then have you ever tried to, you know, to assert yourself in Hollywood?"

"So I end up alone against all the rest?" Alain says. "No thanks."

"What d'you know about that? I'm telling you again, the Hollywood producers aren't all the same. We've got all kinds. We still do, even if money's always taking over creation and cinema. Look at Lawrence Bender, you know, Tarantino's producer. You think he works exactly like Bruckheimer?"

"Oh, I can't say."

"Oh, come on. You see our blockbusters, that's what you said."

"Yes, but I've never attended any of their shootings and postproduction works."

"If everybody had to know about everything... You don't need to."

"I never tell about things I don't know about. If you don't mind I'll see later about some transfer. If the film fails at the box-office, it will be kind of difficult anyway. What about you, haven't you thought about settling here, in France?" Alain asks, suddenly.

"Are you all right?" Tony says, surprised.

"I'm fine."

"You're losing it. I don't speak French, and your movies can't be exported to us anyway."

"Can you explain me why? Of course they can be, you just don't wanna buy them. Except of course when they first meet great success here. You'd rather 'remake' our films as well as those from Spain, Italy and Asia, instead of distributing them across your territory."

"What can I do? Most Americans think there's nothing and nobody beyond our coasts and borders. They don't even have a passport."

"And you don't do much for this to change and for your fellow citizens to evolve a little bit."

"I ain't no geography teacher."

"Very funny."

"That's a fact."

"Or as I said before you're all scared to death. That's why you need to 'americanize' everything in sight, you know, to remake every successful foreign language film you can find and make it look American. You're too scared to discover any culture that is superior to yours. Or you just don't want to understand the world because you believe your country is the whole world."

"Make it simple. Maybe we just believe that a foreign language movie can't be a hit in our country."

"Yeah!" Alain almost startles. "Of course. The money. *That*'s the reason. Always the money. For you, everything that is not American can't bring big big dollars."

"Okay, Mister I-know-everything, you are so bright about us Americans, what do you suggest?" Tony asks, sarcastic. "Don't be shy, tell me."

"Well," Alain suggests, "first you could settle here to change the way your colleagues and fellow citizens think."

"Do you really mean that? Me, settling in France?"

"Like Johnny Depp, yes. Why not?"

"Johnny Depp lives in France only because he married a French girl," Tony retorts.

"So what?"

"Don't be silly."

"I'm not asking you to marry a French girl. I mean you could produce a couple of our films, you know, this way they will be taken more seriously by your system, they could be distributed in your country. That would be some kind of starting."

"To the end of my career, yes."

"Don't be silly."

"If I was a nabob that would be very possible," Tony explains with a grin, "and I'll probably accept with great pleasure. Unfortunately I'm not a nabob and despite my resume I'm not powerful enough. You understand?"

"Not very well."

"Look, it wouldn't work anyway, your

film wouldn't pass your borders. Forget about it."

"Okay. I'll ask Bruckheimer or Zanuck, or David Brown, or Spielberg, for the service."

"Shit." Tony sighs, shaking his head. "Look, I'll think about it, okay?"

"Especially if this project is a box-office blast."

"Yeah. Especially in that case."

"You'll become a nabob then."

"Okay. Please forget about it now."

"I mean it, man. A love story, taking place in Paris, the most romantic city in the world, your fellow citizens will be melting down on this, they'll love it."

"Yeah."

"James Cameron will have no choice but give up."

"What's the matter with you?"

"Haven't you ever felt optimistic in your life?"

Tony's cell phone rings.

"I'd rather say you're being kind of hysterical. It won't last long." He takes the communication. "Hello?" There's a beat. "Oh... all right. Send him up." He cuts.

"What's going on?" Alain asks.

"The director is coming."

"What? You told me you pretended to talk to him on the phone."

"I lied."

"If you keep lying to your co-workers, you'll never be a nabob in your life."

"Because you believe you need to tell the truth to succeed in this business?"

"Of course!"

"Let me tell you this, when you're a producer in Hollywood you have to lie all the time. Especially to the screenwriters, to make them believe that their stories are good when they're not." He picks up the script. "Look at this one, it's a piece of shit and it's being produced."

"What did you say to the writer?"

"You guess!"

"Maybe the director is good."

"We'll check it out."

"I saw his short film. Believe me, he's got talent."

"I'll check it out. Maybe."

"If he is good, and I believe he is, the film will be good too. And even if it's not, it could work anyway, bring much money."

"Yeah, and I'll become a nabob."

"That's right. Me too."

"Great."

"There are many bad films that have worked very well."

"Of course," Tony says, looking at him.

"Look at *The Da Vinci Code.* What a waste!"

There's a pause. "Why are you trying to make me so comfortable?" Tony finally asks. "You're not talking to some stupid chick. Why don't you tell me what you really believe, that I'm just a lousy producer from Hollywood, who only thinks about the dough and produces nothing else but shitty movies?"

"Hey, if you're a lousy producer, then so am I," Alain retorts. "We're working together on this thing."

"Yeah, but at least you didn't read the script completely."

"So what? You think that makes me better than you? You're working with full knowledge of the facts, when I'm not. Hasn't it come through your mind that I could be here only for the opportunity and profit?"

"We've already talked it over, and it's your problem. If you wanna buy me flowers, you'll do that after the film is released, and only if it works." Somebody knocks on the door. "It's him I guess."

"I'll open it," Alain says. He stands up, walks to the door and as he opens it Tony stands up and walks to the door.

There's a young man standing in the doorway. Joe Coons. The director.

"Mr. Coons?" Alain asks him.

"Yes," Coons replies.

"Come on in." Coons comes in and they shake hands. "How are you doing?" Alain asks him.

"Okay."

Tony comes close to him and shakes hands with him.

"Nice to meet you, mister Coons."

"Thanks. So, what did you bring me here for?" Coons asks Tony.

"Oh, we have to discuss a little bit about the film."

"Are you sure it's the good place for that?"

"Don't you think so? Don't worry about it anyway. I suppose you know how you intend to film the story?"

"Hopefully I do, it's part of my job."

"Let's go have a seat," Alain says. He points at his desk. "My desk is right here."

"Mine is right here," Tony says, pointing at his desk.

"It's not your desk," Alain says back to him.

Tony doesn't pay attention. Both Alain and him walk to their respective desks, Coons doesn't know where to go.

"Come here, Coons," Tony says to him.

"No, here," Alain says. "Take this chair."

Tony walks to Coons and takes him to 'his' desk. "Have a seat."

Alain sighs with annoyance without showing any. He finally picks up his own chair and walks with it to his partner's desk.

Tony and Coons have a seat, Alain puts his chair beside Coons and does the same.

"Okay, mister…" Tony begins.

"You can call me Joe, if you like."

"Okay, Joe… what do you personally think of the story?"

"It's a classical romance. Not *Pretty Woman,* but almost."

"*Pretty Woman* is about Cinderella turned into some crude hooker. This script is not exactly that kind."

"It's still about a poor girl's affair with a golden boy and shit."

"The poor girl is not poor. She's from the middle class."

"Ain't it the same?" Coons asks.

"Not exactly," Tony answers, slightly shaking his head.

"I don't agree."

"Whatever," Alain says.

"There's a difference between middle class and low class," Tony argues.

"Sure," Coons says.

"The girl's parents have regular jobs."

"Yes, but she doesn't have one herself. She has no money."

"That doesn't mean she's poor."

"Sure it does. I'm talking about her only. Screw the class."

"Okay," Tony says, surprised. "Whatever."

"What do you wanna tell him exactly?" Alain asks Tony.

"I'm coming to it." To Coons: "You see, we have our own idea about how we want this shot and made."

"Really?" Coons asks.

"Yes. Have you seen such films before? You know… love films?"

"Sure."

"What kinds of films do you like?"

"Is this that important?"

"Yes."

"I like all kinds. All I ask is a movie to be interesting, whatever the genre."

"Do you like the Hollywood style?"

"There's no Hollywood style. There's just Hollywood."

There's a pause.

"Believe me, there *is* a Hollywood style," Tony confirms. "I'm sure you know about it, and we'd like you to shoot the film this way."

"I see."

"This is gonna be your first feature, so I wanted to be straight with you about it."

"I guess you are."

"He'll always be standing behind you on set, to make sure you do," Alain says ironically.

"Not always," Tony retorts.

"Can you tell me a little bit about that style?" Coons asks Tony.

"It can't be explained," Tony responds.

"Is it taught in schools?"

"I guess not. It's taught all by itself, on the job."

"I guess it's the style that brings money and success, right?"

"I suppose so."

"My basic job is to do cinema," Coons says.

"Sure. I didn't say it was not."

"Okay. So what you're talking about is not really my business."

"Sure it is. You'll find out later. Trust me about it."

"Are you a film fan, mister?" Coons asks.

"If I was, I guess I'd be a filmmaker, just like you."

"And you're telling me about some style?"

"Easy. I didn't teach you anything about any style."

"But you're asking me to forget about my way to do films. Did you see my short, mister?"

"I have to admit I didn't."

"Do you wanna see it?"

"No."

"Why not?"

"We don't see short films."

"Of course."

"I've seen it, and it's a good film, you know," Alain says.

"I'm sure it is," Tony approves.

"Thanks anyway," Coons says.

"Well, Joe… I wish you good luck."

"No success?"

Tony grins. "Not now. Maybe later."

"Thanks anyway," Coons says again. "Now if you excuse me… I need to go talk to some crew members."

"I'm leaving with you. I need a cigarette anyway."

"I'm leaving too," Alain says.

"Are you sure?" Tony asks him, grinning some more.

"Yeah, I'm sure."

They all stand up, ready to leave.

"So you do see short films?" Coons asks Alain.

"Yeah," Alain says to him. "I don't work in Hollywood."

Coons shows some smile. "My agent does both."

"Yeah...?"

"He works in Hollywood and he sees short films."

"He must be a great guy," Tony says, sniffing a little.

"He just doesn't work in one of those big studios."

Coons leaves the office first. Soon Alain and Tony follow, picking up their stuff first. Alain lets Tony out, and as he's about to switch off the light and leave, he kind of freezes, remembering Tony's ironic question ('Are you sure?'). And he gets a little bit irritated as he realizes that as soon as Coons had entered the room,

Tony hadn't paid any more attention to Alain, as if he hadn't been in his own office. All his attention had been focused on Coons and on the way he was reasoning as the director. Alain doesn't take long to understand that Tony would be on set at almost all times and do anything to take control of the film, to have it made the way he wanted it to be made. And it's not part of his intentions to imitate him or be used as his shadow, and to become the kind of Hollywood interfering producer he doesn't like. He still has the possibility to use Coons' phone number that is on the script.

So he changes his mind, closing the door but not leaving his office. He takes his seat behind his desk and turned his laptop computer back on, then he puts his headphones back on his head and continues watching *Les Valseuses* on DVD.

Ten, twenty, thirty minutes… then an hour later, Tony hadn't come back.

And he hadn't called.

From the same author

*CHARLIE'S TRIPS*

www.ingramcontent.com/pod-product-compliance
Lightning Source LLC
Chambersburg PA
CBHW071628140626
46555CB00021B/1251

*9 780956 558015*